MR. PISCES

MR. PISCES

TAYANA THOMPSON

DEDICATION

"Relationships come with lessons some teach you "unconditional love, self-love, boundaries, and patience it's your job to figure out your lesson and learn it."

Table of Contents

I AM WHO I AM

Being a child and becoming a parent is not something a child would dream of, but it's my reality. I was born into the world differently, with extra eyelids and responsibilities destined for me. These elevated expectations have weighed heavily on my life since the very beginning. It became an even better burden when I discovered my spiritual gifts. Yet, I lacked guidance on their usage. I couldn't escape the overwhelming feeling of isolation and being an outcast that consumed my thoughts.

 At an early age, I quickly learned to suppress my true self and be strong. Contain my emotions while still embodying feminine energy. It was frustrating learning, at just 8 years old, how to cook, clean, manage my anger towards men, and cater to others. As a young girl with dark skin and colorful beaded hair flowing past my shoulders, I naturally stood out. I was taller than the average child my age. My grandparents became my parents, as I became a casualty of their battles over my grandfather. May his soul rest in peace. As a child, it was challenging to manage casually, as if my life wasn't already hard enough. One would think that someone would consider that, but unfortunately, they did not. Looking back on it now, I have learned to forgive. I appreciate my parents for giving me life, even amid the challenges we encountered together. Their strength and resilience have shaped who I am today.

Throughout my life, I have been able to ease the burdens of many people, bring peace to their existence, show unconditional and expectant love, heal broken hearts, provide solutions to others' problems, break generational curses, and express gratitude. But please, do not for one moment think I hadn't brought my fair share of pain to others because I did. Hurt people indeed hurt other people. The truth of the matter is pain is your connection to growth. No matter what the experience is, take heed of the lesson. If you don't, you will find yourself in a repeating cycle. Learn to stand in your truth and believe in your truth, no matter what that truth may be. Being the oldest girl on both sides, surrounded by many males, was annoying. They didn't accept my feminine side or respect it. I spent years making others happy, even having children of my own. Three, to be exact, and no. I didn't want any children, but they were here. Motherhood was hard but enduring for me. I gave my children the love and compassion that I hungered for. The father of my children was like my real father, a nightmare. There is an old saying that says women have babies or marry their fathers and I experienced that statement. I gained an understanding of my father's behavior when he was with my mother. Can you say it is narcissistic? This is an understatement because he, like my father, refused to change his behavior and take accountability. As time went on, I came more at ease with single parenthood.

My encounters with men were intriguing and enticing. One day, after a conversation with a stranger, I discovered a mysterious and seductive look about myself. The man mentioned how my eyes communicated without saying a word. This realization was a remarkable gift. It might explain the considerable number of men pursuing me. Although I wasn't entirely sure what it meant, I was determined to find out. While at work, a co-worker suggested I start an online dating profile. I was uncertain but filling out my dating profile. I pressed the finish button. The notifications came in from a variety of different men.

PRINCE CHARMING ISN'T CHARMING

Days before Rachel, the co-worker, came to find Safari to see what type of man had been in her inbox. Rachel referred to Safari, a dating website she had been on for a while. Safari's only concern was attracting the wrong guy. This made Safari question herself. Was she presenting herself wrong? What was the man seeing in her? So, Rachel asked Safari about her experience with the website. Safari brushed the conversation off and went into her office. She didn't want to be detailed about her dating love life with a co-worker at her job. The idea made her dismayed. Safari was keen on maintaining her professional life and personal life separately. The reality was becoming discouraging until she stumbled upon Chris' profile. He was handsome, successful, and seemed like he could be her prince charming. Chris had left her three messages, greeting her with the softest expressions of gratitude.

 The others of them weren't normal. They had a Playboy vibe about themselves. Safari's intuition shouted at her when she scrolled through the messages. Most of the man messages said I am not looking for anything serious without saying it. The messages started with a What's up? Hi beautiful, can you be mine? Can we meet today, and where is your man? These greeting messages were red flags for her. She made a "Something to Do List" and placed them on it. This made Safari question the dating pool. The drastic change in people's behaviors and communication styles had diminished from when she was single. She was up for the challenge despite her worries. Safari messaged Chris back, and they hit it off right away. After going back and forth for a week, Safari agreed to meet Chris for coffee. She dashed home from work to shower and put on her favorite black dress. This dress hugged every part of Safari's body in the right way. The dress complimented her legs and booty extremely effectively. Safari pulls up to the coffee shop before she gets out. She sprays her perfume once over her neck and two sprays per wrist. She had just bought that new Alien perfume and the scent turned heads. She goes ahead to the front entrance of the coffee shop. She spots Chris sitting at a table. She cannot see whom he is talking to because of his body movements. Safari enters the shop and spots Chris sitting at a table with another woman. He placed his right hand over her left. Safari's mouth drops wide open at once. She retreats into a corner at the eye length of the two. The server stops her dead in her tracks, greets her, and asks her to take her order. Safari tells her to come back until she figures out what she wants. The server retreats to the counter. The nerve of this guy Safari muffles. Did he double-book? Why would he do such a thing? Was another question going through her mind? Her intuition screamed, should I teach him a valuable lesson or walk away? She was furious at this point. He had not thought of checking his watch for the time or anything. Her presence captivated him, for sure. This was pulling on Safari's heartstrings. The server walked back toward her, and Safari confidently placed her order. "Coffee, please. Make it piping hot with no creamer or sugar. Thank you, ma'am," she replied. Without hesitation, she strode over to the table where Chris and the woman were engaged in a quiet conversation.

OUTRIGHT IN THE OPEN

The coffee shop was semi-crowded. Safari had the devil and angel on her shoulder. The angel said, "Do not react without gaining clarity the angel said. The devil refuted no scold that butt he deserves it." In the background, there was low chatter. The clicking of her heels echoed throughout the shop. Chris still had not peered up from looking in her direction. She approaches the table with her purse and cup in her hand. She was standing dead in the middle of both. Chris was on her left; the lady was on her right. Safari cleared her throat, which snapped Chris out of a glaze. He glances up and jumps to his feet withdrawing his hand from the lady's hand. Chris said, "What is going on? Wait, let me explain. It is not what it looks like." The lady gathers her things while nodding her head back and forth. Safari interrupts her and says, "No, sweetie, you stay because I am sure as hell going. "Next, she turned to Chris and said, do not bother, just lose my number loser, and headed towards the exit. The server runs right over in their direction. Safari says, "I am leaving." There is nothing to worry about. The spectators in the coffee shop started whispering and shaking their heads in astonishment. She was proud of herself for not acting out or pouring coffee. When Safari was inside the car, she yanked out her phone, changed his name in her contacts to "Fullofit", and blocked him. When she got home, Safari took a bottle of her favorite wine from her stockpile, poured herself a glass, and logged onto a dating website to check her messages. She needed light-hearted entertainment from the earlier incident. A good laugh before heading to bed would soothe her soul. Her day had been long. She was looking forward to the weekend and was excited it was Friday. Scrolling through endless messages, one caught her eye. She clicked on his profile because the background of the photos spoke volumes about him. The abstract artwork he was standing beside drew me into him that night. He was handsome, with a rough edge. We talked all night after responding to his first message. The next day Brian sent his number and told her to call him when she got time. She locked the number in her phone and went on with her day. She called to check on him later that night. The phone rang once, and he answered. Safari introduced herself, and the conversation continued until the early morning hours. They talked about family, relationships, heartbreaks, funny moments, and even offered a meet and greet, but Safari declined because of scheduling issues. Safari knew that working over forty hours a week, attending school full-time, raising three children, and maintaining a social life at the bar. The tantalizing thought danced within her mind; a dangerous temptation beckoning her to explore. Their conversations flowed seamlessly, magnetizing with unspoken desires, echoing through the weeks like untold secrets in the night skies.

Finally, Super Bowl weekend came, and Safari found herself in full surrender mode. The promise of the meet and greet with Brian lit her honey wound ablaze, an opportunity to bask in his presence. He captivated her with his words, each syllable drawing her in like honey to a bee. She was not afraid to dive in headfirst, heart and all. As a Pisces, he exuded an aura of mystery and creativity. His every gesture embodied the fluidity of water.

She had prepared a fiesta taco bar, the spicy aroma wafting through the air while sending the children to their grandparents. Safari's excitement and nerves peek after reminiscing slightly about the incident at the coffee shop that lingered in her mind. The clock inches toward seven o'clock, and her heart races. She paces back and forth, her palms slick with anticipation.

Just then, her phone rang, jolting her from her thoughts. She slipped into her room, her heart pounding, and grabbed the phone from the nightstand. It was Brian calling. She answered breathlessly, feeling a magnetic pull towards him.

"It's Brian," his voice flowed over the line, low and inviting. "I'm at the door," he said, his voice low and inviting.

PERFECTION DOESN'T EXIST

With a surge of adrenaline, Safari bolted towards the front door, her heart pounding in rhythm with her footsteps. As she swung open the door, his cologne enveloped her senses, shocking her with a bolt of electricity. She felt an immense stir of excitement as she took him in—it had been a while since she experienced such a feeling. In his presence, she found a man who stimulated her intellect, and she longed for a mental connection rather than just a physical one. Safari struggled to contain herself because his irresistible smile brought a blush to her cheeks, igniting a warmth from within she had forgotten, even existent within her. Engulfed in the attraction, her senses fired on all cylinders. It had been far too long since she felt such an overwhelming attraction. Safari led him into her home, each step feeling charged with promise. The kitchen awaited, vibrant with the colors and scents of her culinary creation. There was an unspoken connection between them that was visible—an electric charge that filled the air as they shared their passions and hobbies over dinner. Their mutual love for festivals, trying new restaurants, and traveling brought them closer together. Their chemistry blossomed as they savored a glass of wine afterward, reminding them of the beauty of genuine connections. Safari couldn't quite put her finger on what drew her to him, but the chemistry was undeniable. He was different—his confident presence and playful banter ignited something deep within her. The conversation flowed effortlessly. Every word left her speechless. With each glance, she could feel the heat building between them. When they reached the door, the air was thick with anticipation. He leaned in, his lips brushing against hers, and nose gently touching hers in a kiss that ignited her senses and left her breathless. She could not wait to see him again. The bond between Brian and Safari grew stronger after that night. The following months flew by, and their communication deepened. Their daily routines intertwine, filled with family nights and date nights. Brian brought her immense happiness.

While preparing for work, Brian's phone rings. He stumbles to answer it but declines the call. Seconds later, it rang again, and Brian ignored it once more. Concerned, Safari asked if everything was okay. Brian replied with a sly smile, "Yes." Curiosity piqued; Safari inquired about the meaning behind his expression. Rather than responding, Brian walked into another room.

Although Safari tried not to judge him, she could not shake the feeling that Brian's behavior seemed off. His actions left Safari questioning his authenticity, sowing seeds of suspicion in her mind. She did not want to relive the pain of her past, nor did she wish to overlook troubling behaviors. Safari understood that no one was perfect, but the uncertainty gnawed at her. "Can I manage his rough edges? Is there someone else? What is he hiding from me?" The questions flooded her mind, each more unsettling than the last.

She decided it was time to address the situation head-on. They needed to talk about boundaries and intentions. After dressing, stepping out to clear, determined to find out if his motives aligned with his words.

Safari tucked the kids into bed, her heart racing with determination. The air in the living room felt thick with unspoken words as she sat across from him, sensing the tension radiating from his body. His eyes darted away when she casually mentioned their earlier conversation about his phone, a flash of unease crossing his face. Safari took a deep breath, creating a non-judgment zone. "Let's talk about everything," she offered softly, her voice steady despite the storm churning inside her. They delved into deep discussions about their needs and set boundaries to allow them to thrive as a couple. Hours slipped by as they exchanged hopes, fears, and desires. In that vulnerable moment, they shared an enthusiastic connection that felt electric, reaching a level of intimacy she thought would erase the shadows between them.

But as everything seemed to settle back into normalcy, a small knot of doubt lingered in Safari's mind.

MEETING THE PARENTS

Safari, a keen observer of family dynamics, was eager to meet Brian's family. Brian was surprised by her children and the connection that blossomed overnight. He wore the father role well. After one year of dating, we achieved a new milestone in their relationship. Today will be the day I meet Brian's family. As we are approaching the location nervousness invades Safari's mind. Brian noticed her facial expression and body language change and asked Safari if everything was okay. She replied, "Yes." Safari never had a problem with her earlier relationship with family members. She did not know what to expect, so she hoped for the best. When they arrived at his mom's house, his mother and grandfather met them with embracing arms. They were a friendly and average family.

The atmosphere shifted as we moved forward. Mrs. Jones engaged in small talk. Meanwhile, Brian's grandfather could not help but draw comparisons between me and the other women he'd dated, making it clear he believed he was out of my league. Attempting to break the awkwardness in the air, Mrs. Jones launched a collection of off-color jokes, each landing with nervous laughter and incredulity.

We gathered around the table, and the atmosphere crackled with warmth and tension. Dinner began with laughter and chatter, but soon his mother shifted the conversation toward Brian's involvement in the lives of his siblings and their children. With a knowing tone, she hinted at Brian's questionable dating history, which caused him to make an unfamiliar face that intrigued me and made me want to question its meaning.

I discovered Brian had spent his life looking up to his uncles and grandfather. However, their infamous womanizing and deceitful ways left a mark of disdain for women. Safari shot him at a concerned glance, her brow furrowing as she sensed the turmoil within him. Brian squirmed in his seat, turning unusual colors and sweating. Safari could see that the anguish was unmistakable—a storm brewing behind his eyes. Or was one of his reactions a performance because of exposure?

Brian, no longer able to cope with the intense and volatile dinner, exists hastily. Safari attempted to follow him. Mrs. Jones gestures for her to allow him alone time. Then she reveals to her Brian's reluctance to pursue women his age because of a heartbreaking experience from his past. Saying my son had fallen in love with a promiscuous woman before meeting me. This woman also had a baby, and he loved and cared for the child, doing everything he could, even watching over the baby while she cheated. The young lady deceived and broke his heart, shattering him to pieces. So, he vowed to seek a more mature partner. I was in awe of this loss for words. Why didn't Brian tell me about this? Oh, we will talk about this later in bed, Safari thought.

His defensiveness now made sense to her. Despite the challenges, Safari gives her boyfriend and his family a chance. She knew they cared for one another despite their issues. Safari was determined to support Brian and help him work through his traumas. Her love for Brian fostered deep patience within her. She did not want Brian to take her kindness for granted. Safari's sensitivity to people's struggles made her understand, patient, and affectionate.

Her phone buzzed incessantly, interrupting the family time; it was her mother. Knowing it was time to leave, Safari answered her mom's call. When her mom asked where she was, Safari replied, "I'm on the way." She hangs up and walks towards the exit, informing Brian's mom that she must go. Mrs. Jones accompanied her outside. As Safari approached the parked car, she noticed Brian sitting inside, his attention absorbed by his phone. She suddenly opened the car door, inadvertently startling him. He jumped out, and Safari quickly signaled that she needed to gather the children. After hugging his mom, Brian climbed into the car and drove away. They both turned to bid farewell to his mother, but an unshakeable feeling lingered in the air. Safari noticed a subtle change in Brian's behavior.

A chilling breeze swept through the air, leaving nothing but idle minds to roam. Not a word escaped either of their lips. Exhaustion weighed heavily on Safari, and she desperately needed to rest. Brian's embarrassment consumed him, causing his mind to race. After that day, Brian's once-loving texts turned silent. He became secretive, and Safari could not quite put her finger on it, but something fell off. Their communication was as dry. Brian's hours at work increased, and he spent more time with friends than with her.

BRIAN

The sun gleamed through the window, obstructing Brian's view as he grasped the visor to pull it down. His job schedule was erratic, and his time felt stifling. He developed a newfound enthusiasm for life. Three remarkable children—Tim, Tina, and Tammy— had entered his world and transformed his perspective. Their laughter filled the air like music, each giggle and squeal reminding him of the beauty in simple moments. Their presence contributed to Brian's growth, offering a sense of peace and bliss he had never encountered. He felt empowered. The unconditional love healed various parts. With the children by his side, he appreciated the trivial things—a game of tag in the playground, or even the prayers before bedtime. Their unconditional love wrapped around him like a warm blanket, healing parts of him wounded and battered over the years. He vowed to the children that he would never hurt or harm them, and he intended to keep that promise.

However, his relationship with their mother remained uncertain after a strenuous dinner with his family. He was confident she would not take the children away from him. Brian was unsure about the current state of their relationship because of his fear of losing her. The dinner had been unfortunate; his mother revealed things he had asked her not to, and his grandfather displayed his usual spontaneity. Unable to bear it, Brian left and sat in the car. As he drove home, the silence in the car felt oppressive. Not being able to discern her thoughts and the silence terrified him. The quietness was so thick that if there were crickets, you could hear them. The fear of hearing the wrong thing prompted him to remain silent. Instead of spending the night with her, he went home. That night, they disconnected from one another. A whirlwind filled his mind, leaving him unclear about her feelings.

Reflecting on how hard he had worked to reach this point, that night Brian logged into the dating site once at home and scrolled through his old messages with Safari. Fear of rejection clouded his judgment. He found himself captivated by her profile picture, but her eyes stood out to him. Her eyes pulled him deeper into her. He hailed from the Midwest and with various complex women, but none compared to her.

It was a quiet evening when he sent her a message—sweet, yet laced with a captivating charm, designed to draw her in. He watched his screen, heart skipping a beat, and awaited her reply. But three days stretched into a week with unspoken words and possibilities.

He knew he was nice-looking—those compliments floated around him like the scent of cologne—but he understood that something with his look triggered her to hesitate. No, it was something unspoken but alluring. His ego, like his meticulously selected wardrobe, filled any space he entered. There was an alpha male technique he would do that caused women to flutter around him like moths to a flame.

Her response arrived—sharp and calculating. Delivering warmth, catching Brian off guard, and deflating his ego. Her words reflected doubts about him, creating a twist that left him reeling. Undeterred, he crafted another smooth line, convinced that this would break through her defenses. But this time, three days stretched into two weeks later, she repelled him with the same consequence—her words just as direct, her intentions just as blunt. She dodged his advances, unraveling the bravado he had carefully built. Her bluntness stung; she declared her distaste in a Playboy. Yes, he had a part of his life dedicated to that image, but the depths of his being unrecognized within himself. I knew I possessed powers that could induce a love trance in women. It was a gift from the Creator. I am a magician, and a higher power has granted this right to me. What can I say? My existence speaks volumes. I can put you in a trance without you even realizing it. The frequency of my voice can compel you to follow my rules. The intensity in my gaze, swift and striking like lightning, can persuade you to fulfill them. I am aware of my power, and I stand confidently in it.

He remembered her messages vividly, replaying each moment in his mind. The way she articulated her disinterest was both enlightening and humbling. It was as if she held up a mirror to him, not just his persona, but the wounds he had concealed. She shot down his advances with love, honesty, and a clarity that struck deep.

As he relived those moments, the thrill of the chase drifted into memory, leaving him longing, intrigue, and respect for the woman who had challenged his perception.

A month went by, and various back-and-forth messages, to convince Safari of my friendly guy's personality. Her disenchantment sucked me into a deeper tailspin. I needed help, so I called my mother for advice about Safari. I followed my mother's advice. Finally, she agreed to have dinner with me but at her home. The rest was history. We were inseparable. I was a gentleman in public, but a beast in the sheets. My spirit craved her. This was strange for me, being that I rarely had to put work towards women.

Here I was in my head, avoiding Safari. I finally got her to get comfortable with me and open. We did everything as a couple. My old ways were burdening me. Women's attention for me heightened to an unimaginable level. My avoidance and little conversation only over text messages with Safari became a strain. I was dating a vast number of gorgeous women behind her back. It was as if women's attraction levels for me increased drastically. The town we were in was small, so I strategized my steps. My anxiety level was through the roof, but the sensation I got from sneaking was addictive. An indescribable rush shot through my body.

WHAT A DAY

Tim's defiance about getting out of bed and Tina's irritated reaction put me on edge. Was there something in the air this morning? The responses of others also disturbed me. It was exhaustion from the day before. My relationship with Brian felt unbalanced. A week had passed since I last heard from him. Then he texted, proposing to take the children to the park. I replied, "Sure." He avoided me, but I sympathized with his relationship with the kids. His refusal to enter the house when he dropped off the children upset me, but I tried to shrug it off and started preparing dinner. A decision about our relationship was brewing in my mind.

Traffic was chaotic, as usual. When I finally entered the building, the rain hung thick. I made it to my office, drenched and overwhelmed by the downpour. Settling into my chair, I frowned at the piled-up on my desk. I placed my cell phone and lunch inside the desk and tackled my workload.

Thirty minutes had stretched into what felt like an hour. My cell phone rang incessantly inside my desk, the vibrations messaging against my outer thigh like an annoying massager. The piles of paperwork were my only focus; I was determined to get this paperwork down to a reasonable amount. Each pulse was like an urgent heartbeat beneath the clutter, but I pushed through, shunning the static, drowning out my productivity.

The phone repeats its relentless summons. Whispering distractions threatened to pull me from my work. As the morning slipped by, I found solace in my rhythm, enveloped in the smooth melodies of my R&B playlist that wrapped around me like a comforting cocoon. When the clock finally hit noon, I grabbed my lunch and extracted my phone from the depths of my work drawer before making my way toward the lunch cafeteria. My thoughts flitted between the mundane and the dramatic, but nothing could prepare me for the surge of emotion that awaited.

I glanced at my phone. The moment I did, it felt as if a semi-truck hit me. My heart was racing, dislodging my breath. I looked at my screen and saw the missed calls and messages from my friend, the one who always had reliable information about everyone in town. Her credibility has always been rock-solid, and the urgency of her latest message sent a chill down my spine. As I read, "Call me right away. It is urgent!"

My dreadful confirmation: *Brian was out with another girl. * The words echoed in my mind, crashing against the walls I had built around my day. The lunchroom noise faded, and only one thought surged through me—what had happened?

I dialed the number, my hands shaking with fury as anger surged. Receiving no answer, I messaged: "Girl, what is happening?" I received your message. Please call me back. I left a voice message. Call me back." My nerves were skyrocketing; hunger replaced itself with the pain of uncertainty. "Why isn't she calling me back? Speaking quietly to myself. I checked my contacts, and dialed Brian's number, but reached voicemail, so I left a message. I followed up with a message, asking for a call at his earliest opportunity. A co-worker across the room broke my concentration and asked if everything was okay. I replied, yes, just a minor emergency I said. She rubbed my shoulder before returning to her table.

I put my food away and wondered if Brian knew someone had spotted him in town. I waited for Brian or my friend to respond. The clock seemed to drag. My patience was wearing thin. I left work early on a mission to find out the truth. While making a sharp left turn into my driveway, my phone rang.

I looked down and saw Brian's number flashing across the screen. I rushed to answer and turned off the car. Calmly with a sweet phone, I asked him to come to the house because we needed to talk. He agreed to meet me when he gets off work. I was determined to stay calm. Five minutes after getting off the phone with Brian, my friend called. As soon as I answered, she began spilling the tea.

THE CONFRONTATION

Safari paces the living room floor, her heels clicking against the hardwood like a ticking bomb ready to explode. "How could you do that?" she screams at Brian, gas-faced. She called her mom beforehand and arranged for her to keep the children so they could communicate without disturbances. Her palms swung back and forth in frustration.

Brian pauses; his hands buried in his pockets as a lost stare spread across his face. The details of his discretion repeat in her mind. A woman with long, flowing hair and a stunning, structured figure at the summer Italian Festival, where Brian had held her hand, shared refreshments, and even kissed her.

Brian did not know what to think. He was silent as a mouse, embodying the stereotype of an emotionally disconnected man. When Safari asked if he had anything to share, he replied, "No." When she pressed him further, asking, "Are you certain?" he hesitated before responding, "Maybe I do."

His unsteady hands and perspiration beaded his forehead. The concerns unraveled in his mind. "The dinner pushed me away from you," Brian admitted. "That day haunts me because I didn't know how you felt afterward." Safari paused and asked, "Why didn't you just ask?" He replied, "I didn't know how to ask." Safari urged him to continue. And he confessed to managing the situation poorly and acted immaturely. Safari then asked Brian if he had been pursuing another woman. Silence filled the room for a moment. "Hello, did you not hear what I just asked you?" she pressed. Brian responded, "Yes, I heard you." Anguish spread through Safari as she processed his answer. His silence conveyed so much more. Resentment arose within Safari as Brian admitted to communicating with other women online.

Resentment arose within Safari as Brian admitted to communicating with other women online. Still, his intention was not to cheat. He was lonely and distracted. She could not understand why he would do that. Trust was hard to build up with her. The words she heard disturbed Safari. She realized the truth, and she had to acknowledge his sincerity. Tears cascaded down Safari's face. The confrontation turned her entire world upside down. Her babies had developed an attachment to him. Their bond was heart-melting. How would she tell her babies about this? They may need therapy after this one, Safari suggested. Brian apologized and assured her never to do it again. But could she depend on him to keep his word? Brian fell to his knees in a desperate plea. A picture of him kissing another woman was all she could imagine. She sent Brian elsewhere that evening. Safari belt with infidelity in her prior relationship and vowed not to do it again. In the upcoming weeks, Safari directed her attention to her children and professional life. Brian's became a distant memory.

Resentment grew within Safari when Brian admitted to communicating with other women online. He said his intentions were not to cheat; he was simply lonely and distracted. Safari struggled to understand why he would engage in such behavior since trust had been hard to establish between them. His words disturbed her. She acknowledged his sincerity, but the pain was too much to bear. Tears streamed down her face as the confrontation turned her world upside down.

Her children had developed a father's relationship with Brian, and their bond was heartwarming and unbreakable. How could she explain this situation to them? She wondered if they might need therapy to cope with the aftermath. Brian apologized, providing reassurance to her. But could she rely on him to keep his word? In desperation, Brian fell to his knees, pleading for forgiveness. Yet, all she could envision was him kissing another woman. The question is, does a zebra ever change its stripes and get cheetah print patterns?

That evening, she asked Brian to leave. Having experienced infidelity in a previous relationship, she had vowed never to go through that kind of pain again. For the next few weeks, Safari focused on her children and her professional life, allowing Brian to become a distant memory. He would call, but she would decline his calls. After weeks of not returning his calls or answering, Brian eventually stopped reaching out. She had abandoned the idea of reconciling with him entirely. Just hearing his name made her feel nauseous; she could not shake the thought of him being with other women while he was with her.

Months went by, and one late night, around midnight, Safari's phone rang. "Who is calling me at this time of night?" she exclaimed in irritation. She had just pulled a double shift, and her body was exhausted. Grabbing her phone, she glanced at the unknown number and answered it. It was Brian, calling her from an out-of-town number. After trying to contact her, he decided to move away.

PHONE CALL

His tone is hoarse. The uncertainty in his speech was a plea escaping his lips like a rushing of flowing water. "I'm sorry, Safari," Brian said on the phone. Life wasn't going as he had expected. Silence followed afterward. He responded, "I see you are," but before he could finish, I blurted out, "What do you want?"

Hesitating before responding, Brian said, "You are still furious with me." Yes, I was, but I chose not to discuss it. Time helped me heal from the pain. He continued, "I miss the kids and you." Disturbed by his frankness, I reacted, "If that's true, did you miss us when you stepped out on me?"

Silence lingered until Brian asked about the children's whereabouts. I missed our conversations and his gentle touch. The deception was still weighing heavily on my mind. I suggested he take more time to reflect and allow me to practice forgiveness.

Our talk ended, and I told him to take care of himself. I hung up the phone and fell asleep. Memories from the past with Brian entered my head space. The sound of my phone alarm disrupted my sleep. Sluggishness and eagerness were disturbing my morning. While driving to work, every love and heartbreak song played on the radio station. Was the universe signaling something to me? I didn't want to disregard the signs in front of me. My thoughts tugged at my heartstrings. It was difficult for me to concentrate on work. Questions invaded my mind about Brian. Why did he call? What did he want? Why did he move elsewhere? He was invading my heart and mind. Was I over him, and did I need male attention? I finished work early and headed home. My exhaustion level was high. Rest was calling my name. My head hit my soft pillow, and my phone rang. An unknown number came across the phone screen. I opted out of answering it and concentrated on resting.

While sleeping, I fall into this dark space. A man appears in a squared spot surrounded by bars, crying. I tried to focus on his face, but it was a blur. Grief and despair surrounded the atmosphere. The man urged me to come closer to him. My eagerness to discover who he was and why I saw him powered my intuition. My inner voice screams to be careful and not to get close. I approached him, putting one foot in front of the other. My inner voice screams stopped. I stop, and he pauses and raises his head toward me. My heart hits the floor in shock. The face I once saw was no longer blurry. I was in disbelief. The orange jail jumpsuit, with bloodshot red eyes, invaded my head space. The questions were spurring out of my mouth. What are you doing here? What happened to you? Tears streamed down my face. I was in awe. I never imagined seeing him in this situation.

He opens his mouth to answer my questions. My son wakes me

from my slumber. I soaked in a puddle of sweat underneath my sheets. Springing to my feet, I ran into the bathroom. Then turn on the shower water and begin showering. Seeing Brian in jail bothered me. I did not know his situation and what was happening in his life, but the scenery kept replaying in my mind. Night came, and Brian was still on my mind. I was contemplating calling him and asking. Instead, I let it go. At three-forty-five in the morning, my phone rang. I looked down and saw a jail number. I was stuck in this dream state.

YOU NEVER KNOW

I have alienated myself from Brian for months. My life was going easy. The operator told his location and that this call was on a recorded line. I said "hello" and went crazy. Drained by not having enough sleep. Brian kept quiet as he allowed me to speak. I can sense the uneasiness in his voice as he waits for me to stop ramping and raging, pausing in between breaths. I reminded myself that we were not in a relationship. His problem was not my problem, but his heartstrings tugged at my heartstrings as he paraphrased the incident. The police officers arrested him and surrounding people that night. Brian had been up for 24 hours partying and joking around with his relatives and friends. A big brawl ensues when the relative gets into an intense argument involving money owed to him. Brian's relative pulls out his gun, and they exchange punches. Neighbors hear the dispute and the exchange of gunfire and call the police. The police show up, and everyone involved goes to jail. A relative friend ended up hospitalized due to an injury that occurred at the incident. There was Brian, sitting in a cell after sacrificing himself for a relative. Brian took the charges and pleaded because of the criminal history the relative previously had. I did not question his decision to self-sabotage. Instead, I offered my helping hand. I could not allow him to rot in a cell after dreaming about the incident before it occurred. The call abruptly ends. I tried to relax in bed, but my mind fought against me. I was tossing and turning back and forth. My mind raced, invading any peace I had before Brian called. Sleep would not allow me to own it. The dream of Brian being in a cell and the anguish I felt owned my spirit. I got out of bed and grabbed my cell phone and laptop. Up at eight in the morning leaving voicemails and researching laws. The children were not in school because of a faculty day. I was making phone calls to attorneys for counsel.

Brian's situation did not look good after speaking with various attorneys who said a 5 to 10-year stay in prison would be a justified plea. Hell, the news terrified me. At night, around eight, my phone rang. I picked up the phone. Brian asked if I could find out the legal options and here, I was, half asleep, delivering him the worst news of his life. I gave him advice from different attorneys. Silent followed when hearing the news. He was waiting to go to court when I talked to him. We did not know the cost of bail. He was silent for a while before expressing gratitude and ending the call.

The news caused his voice to become shaken, and then he rushed off the phone. After the call, I wondered what his night had been like after I told him his fate. A couple of days later, bail had been set. The relative flaked out on him. Brian's was crushed, but he didn't have time to mourn. Weeks and months went by, and our relationship grew stronger. We were working on our future, and he apologized for his actions. He was coming back after six months of being gone. We had agreed to give our relationship another chance. Was this a moral decision for me? Did I forgive Brian for his discretion? These questions weighed heavily on my mind, but I never told him about my internal battle.

NEVER SEEN IT COMING

Nervous and anxious about the phone call. Safari was doing 85 in a 55-mile-per-hour lane. She ignored the yellow lights, speeding and merging onto the highway. At 12:46 AM, she pulls into the roundabout of the bus station. Rain penetrates the dark sky. A colorful track jacket reflects through the window, blinding her vision for a minute. Brian stands there, rehearsing what to say. Her presence erases every word from his memory. He watched her open the door and step out, and their eyes locked when she turned around. Time paused during their embrace. His heart pounds as streams of tears fall from both of their eyes. He broke the silence with, "I am sorry for everything. "It is okay, she replied. I forgive you.

Brian had been fortunate enough to be released after a six-month sentence.

It was a tough time for him, and he could not wait. The infidelity crossed her mind but love and lust prevailed. We held each other tightly, entering the car after a long hug. Over the next few weeks, Brian and Safari spent all their time together, having lunch at the lakefront, cooking meals together, and watching movies late into the night. It was mid-evening, and as they sat on the couch watching TV, Safari noticed that Brian had left his phone on the end table. Brian's phone buzzed, and she reached for the phone; she saw a Facebook message from an unfamiliar woman with the profile name "BadbodyTasha." Safari asks him who the girl is. While holding up the phone. Brian's face drops. "I'm sorry," he said. "You weren't supposed to see that," Safari's heart sank. Brian confesses to dating someone while out of town. He met her at a store and had only been talking for weeks before getting incarcerated. Safari's world was falling apart. How could he manage to not tell me about it? She needed to center herself because he was single. The truth stung, and it did not help that there was little trust. He did not know how to correct his mistake. He sat there in silence, watching Safari cry, feeling helpless.

Suddenly, Safari gets up and leaves. Brian sat there, alone with his thoughts, wondering if he had just destroyed the best thing that had ever happened to him. Days turned into weeks, and Safari did not return any of Brian's calls or texts. She had taken the children and herself to her mother's home to stay for a while. He did not know what to do. He had been out for less than three months and ruined it again. One night, as Brian was sitting in the house, feeling sorry for himself, there was a knock at the door. He opened it to find Safari standing there, tears streaming down her face. "I should not have left like that. I just needed time to think." Brian felt a surge of hope. They could still make things work. "I'm sorry too," he said. "I know I messed up. They stayed up all night talking about the girl and ways to fix their relationship.

PLAGUED

Brian returns to his old job. Safari continues to struggle with Brian's infidelity. She despised the love she had for him. It was an unbreakable bond, so she thought. The only issue was a desire for revenge that plagued her. Family and friends suggested she teach him a valuable lesson. Her higher self would not allow it. She never held interest in putting miles on her body. The idea of getting emotional fulfillment from a different man was intriguing. Should I or should not I repeat in her head? She was choosing to ignore it instead of giving in to temptation. Brian cleaned up his toxic behavior, but did he appreciate her this time? She was not enthusiastic about experiencing disappointment. Her guards were up and prepared for war. Hell had no fire when referring to a scorned woman.

The day was long, hot, and stuffy. Safari decides on the long way home to get more alone time. Enjoying the stillness, she pulls up into the driveway. Then she notices her mother, and cousin's car, surrounding the house. Overtaking it by their abrupt appearance she swiftly picked up her handbag and tripped over her feet at the door. Brian stops her dead in her tracks. The door swung open, everyone stood around as Brian grabbed her hand. Then, kneeling on one knee, he reached out for her other hand. Her heart speeds up and skips a beat. Her eyes light up wide with excitement. Was he serious as the words poured out of her mouth? He was serious.

Brian had taken the time to buy two rings and gathered her nearby relatives. Her thoughts drowned out the current scenery. She only heard babble as he spoke. Besides her mom's sniffles from crying tears of joy. Brian's best friend stood beside him with the widest grin, as if he had won the lottery and there she stood, stuck in a trance with her thoughts and flashbacks of the past. Brian's voice blasts her out of her head. Safari, did you hear me? Huh, I said. Will you take me as your husband? She replied yes. Disparity shined through his eyes. He was not sure of her reply. Hell, she was not either. The past two years were rough. Could she do a lifetime with this man? She thought to herself. Should she say yes? After a long pause, she screamed yes and kissed Brian. She was officially engaged to a man she loved with conflicting thoughts. Not to mention trust issues as well. Did she just put herself into some mess? She wondered. Could she get over the pain without self-destructing or self-sabotaging her relationship? She was not sure but determined to live in the moment. She deserved love and happiness. The engagement excited their children. That late evening, they partied, talked, ate well, and danced the night away. There was love in the air. After everyone left, she settled the children in bed. Brian asked, "Why the long pause to answer?" He chuckles and says that he thought she was going to say No. Safari stood in silence drained, and exhausted. Then quietly and effortlessly walks out of the room to shower. As the water hits her head pain, agony, and grief pours from her eyes. A small scream penetrates her jowls. The flashbacks of his discretion haunted her. Brian's voice intruded her space as she opened her eyes to him getting in. Making her rush to shower and leave him in there. She needed time alone to think without him invading her space. His demons were hunting her, and she craved peace.

AVOIDANCE

In the following weeks, she avoided Brian by scheduling dinner dates with friends and co-workers. She even arranged therapy and doctoral appointments for their children and me. She did not know how long she could avoid Brian, but it was a risk she took until she could fix this internal battle within herself. No, she did not tell him about the therapy sessions. It was not his business until she felt comfortable exposing it to him. While talking to the therapist late Friday evening, she had a light bulb that caused her to address the issue. She needed to talk about her emotions to Brian and express her need to regain trust in the relationship. After the session, she drove home and started her weekly chores. Amid folding clothes in the room, Brian enters. Can we talk? He said with his tone laced with suspicion. Safari replied yes. Brian asked, "Do you have something to tell me? Is everything with us fine?" She replied, "Yes, and why would you ask me that?" He pauses first, stares into her dreamy eyes, and grins with the most devious grin she has ever seen. Safari had no clue that Brian had been watching her for the past couple of weeks. Taking notes and studying her as if she were an open book. Her actions surprised Brian. He had always known her to stick to a particular routine every day. Lately, Safari has been busy without time for him. He could not help but wonder why she had changed. Here he was, questioning her about her actions and whereabouts. Do you think

I do not know when something is bothering you? She shrugged her shoulders in disbelief. Brian spots her anxious eyes looking everywhere but, in his direction, knowing she looks people in the eyes while communicating. A shout comes out of his mouth, "Are you cheating on me?" Brian's accusation took Safari aback. Huh! What are you talking about?" she yelled, her voice shaking with emotion. "I am talking about your routine change. Why are you switching up on me? Brian responded, his voice was growing louder. Brian's words hurt and confused Safari. She could not understand why Brian would accuse her of cheating just because she had changed her daily route. She tried explaining the internal battle and exploring new ways of dealing with those issues, but Brian would not listen. Their argument continued for minutes until Safari stormed out of the house, feeling frustrated and uneasy. Safari's reactions frustrated Brian's anger to grow. He was losing patience with Safari, and she knew it. Later that evening, Brian realized he had overreacted. He knew that Safari would not cheat on him and regretted his behavior earlier in the day. He just could not put his finger on the issue at hand. Brian loved her, but did he ruin their relationship for good? He needed to give her and himself time to calm down. The engagement haven't been called off, but there was a storm brewing in paradise. Safari took off in her car for a silent ride. Contemplating how she could talk to Brian without upsetting him. She loved him, but not as much as she loved herself. They had a significant issue in their relationship that needed addressing before marriage. This ride gave her strength, patience, and courage to talk. So, she picked up the phone and dialed his number. He answers after one ring, excited to hear from her. Safari told Brian to come outside in thirty minutes and jump in the car with her so they could talk. Brian said, "Okay" and waited for Safari to pull into the driveway.

MOMENT OF TRUTH

Safari knew she had to save her relationship. Praying that a scenery change would help them work through their issues. She unlocked the car door, and anxiety consumed her headspace. Brian jumps in and gets comfortable in the seat. As Safari drove through the windy roads, Safari could not help but get nervous. She knew that the conversation they were about to have could make or break their engagement. Brian sat beside her; eyes focused on the passing scenery. Safari took a deep breath and started the conversation. "I know we have been having these problems, Brian. Can we talk it through and find a resolution? Brian nodded and replied, "I have been feeling the same way. But it is not just about the problems we are having. It is about how we communicate with each other. We need to learn to listen to and understand each other. Safari nodded in agreement. "You are right, Brian. I have been trying. to work on that, but I know I still have things I need to learn. I want us to communicate openly and honestly with each other." So, I have been seeing a therapist about the infidelity issue. Brian sits in silence, allowing her to continue talking. Safari mentions how the incident hindered her mental state of mind. Brian nodded in agreement. Acknowledging that his actions caused her pain. Then interrupted her by saying "Safari, I have been working on it." She shakes her head in agreement. Then say "But I have issues with trusting you. I know

I agreed to marry you. I do not think I can. Safari's hand reached out to touch Brian's arm. "I want to, Brian. I love you, and I want us to be blissful together. Strengthening our relationship is a priority. Brian nodded, relieved that Safari agreed with him. He took a deep breath and continued the conversation, his voice quiet and serious. "There's something else I want to talk about, Safari. It is something that has been bothering me for a while." Safari looked at him, her eyebrows furrowed. "What is it, Brian?" Brian hesitated for a moment before speaking. "I feel you don't always consider my feelings. It is not cool to over-talk me when I am speaking. Or who can be pettier than the other? Safari was surprised by Brian's comment. He was voicing his opinion. It turned Safari on in ways she could not admit. "I am sorry if I have neglected your feelings Safari replies. I care about you and our happiness. Brian nodded, feeling relieved that Safari was open to hearing his concerns. He took a deep breath and continued the conversation, his voice calm. "Safari, I want us to express our feelings and opinions without getting defensive or angry and work through our issues together, instead of letting them drive us apart." Safari was relieved and grateful for Brian's willingness to accept her honesty. She knew their relationship was not perfect, but he also knew they had something special between them. Brian squeezed Safari's hand and smiled at her, feeling a sense of hope and optimism for their future together. As they drove back home, the tension between them had lifted. They talked and laughed together, enjoying each other's company. That night Safari expressed her love for Brian when she put on a lingerie piece. Slowly seductively seducing his mind when she danced and peeled off a layer at a time. Taking his mind, body, and soul to ecstasy. A night of electrifying, compassion, bonding between the two. They were back on a more positive road and Safari was at ease. She finished her therapy sessions and began planning her wedding. She was going to be a wife.

ABOUT THE AUTHOR

Meet the visionary behind "Mr. Pisces," Tayana Thompson, an enthusiastic advocate for romance, holistic wellness, and paranormal stories. Tayana seamlessly blends a background in romance, spirituality, and nutrition with a deep-rooted commitment to empowering individuals. Tayana has crafted a phenomenal story drawing from her own experience and imparts practical wisdom on navigating this journey called life. Tayana aims to inspire and encourage others to ask questions. Ask for guidance. Embrace a vibrant peaceful existence, unlocking the secrets to encounters and life experiences. Learn that through heartbreak you gain self-awareness, self-worth, and self-growth. Know that no time you spend with someone is wasted time, it's valuable time you just haven't learned the lesson or the blessing the person holds. Learn to "Live Life Love & Learn"